Cover art by Matt Stawicki
First Printing: September 2002
Library of Congress Catalog Card Number: 2001097173

9 8 7 6 5 4 3 2 1

US ISBN: 0-7869-2798-4
UK ISBN: 0-7869-2799-2
620-88617-001-EN

U.S., CANADA,	EUROPEAN HEADQUARTERS
ASIA, PACIFIC, & LATIN AMERICA	Wizards of the Coast, Belgium
Wizards of the Coast, Inc.	P.B. 2031
P.O. Box 707	2600 Berchem
Renton, WA 98057-0707	Belgium
+1-800-324-6496	+32-70-23-32-77

Visit our web site at www.wizards.com

GEN CON IS A REGISTERED TRADEMARK OF GEN CON LLC.

CREDITS

EDITOR
MARK SEHESTEDT

ART DIRECTOR
RYAN SANSAVER

GRAPHIC DESIGN
ROBERT CAMPBELL

TYPESETTING
ROBERT CAMPBELL

PROJECT MANAGER
AARON ALBERG

PRODUCTION MANAGER
CHAS DELONG

contents

Special thanks to all the artists who took time out of their schedule to answer a bunch of questions as well as creating their self-portraits.

FOREWORD

BY margaret weis

One day in 1983, Tracy Hickman sat down with artist Larry Elmore and began to tell him a story. The story was about a wondrous world where dragons vied with each other over who was going to rule mankind, a world where gods walked with mortals and where heroes fought and died in the name of honor, a world where gnomes built steam-powered mousetraps and kender borrowed your handkerchief.

Larry was so entranced and enthralled with the tale that he went home and began to draw some of the characters. In that moment, the vision of Dragonlance and the art that would portray that vision became intrinsically linked.

Many years have passed since the publication of the first *The Art of the Dragonlance Saga*. During those years, the vision has evolved and expanded. New artists have come to portray their own vision of the world. The result is a marvelous collection of many views of Krynn as seen through many different eyes.

Some of the art is from the original artists who first worked on the Dragonlance project: Larry Elmore, Keith Parkinson, Jeff Easley, and Clyde Caldwell. Other pieces are from artists who have come more recently to the world, including Matt Stawicki, Mark Zug, Brom, Daniel Horne, Todd Lockwood, Kevin McCann, Jerry Vander Stelt, and Tim Hildebrandt.

We couldn't include everything, because there is so much great art! We hope you'll find some old favorites in this book, as well as discover some new ones.

~Enjoy!

DRAGONLANCE
AND ITS ARTISTS

BY PETER ARCHER

Art has always been integral to the DRAGONLANCE setting—more so, perhaps, than to almost any other fantasy world. When Tracy Hickman and other designers and editors at TSR were developing the setting in the early 1980s, they turned to artist Larry Elmore. The deadline for their pitch was growing nearer, and they wanted some art to make their case more impressive. Elmore was enthused by the idea and produced in a single weekend the conceptual paintings that defined the major characters in the story.

In late 1983, Margaret Weis, newly hired as a book editor by TSR, joined the design team on the project. After attempting to find an author for the novel series that would accompany the project, Weis suggested to Hickman that the two of them try their hand at writing the series. They spent a weekend writing the prologue and first five chapters to *Dragons of Autumn Twilight*. The rest is history. The novel became a best-seller and was followed by its two sequels, launching DRAGONLANCE into fantasy history.

My own involvement in the series began in the spring of 1996, when I was hired by TSR, based in Lake Geneva, Wisconsin, as managing editor of the Book Publishing department. I rapidly came to know, through correspondence and later, at the GEN CON® game fair, in person, many of the wonderful authors who made up the DRAGONLANCE world: Rick Knaak, Jean Rabe, Chris Pierson, Doug Niles, Jeff Grubb, Nancy Berberick, Paul Thompson, and Tonya Cook, to name just a few. I also met many of the artists who contributed to the series and quickly learned to appreciate their ability to leave their unique mark on the world of Krynn.

The Book Department, in those days, was in a dark corner of TSR's headquarters, jammed under some stairs. Appropriately enough, this area was referred to as "Siberia." Up the stairs and down a corridor was the staff artists' studio, jammed with easels, paints, costumes for models, and general clutter. In the midst of it, one could usually find Jeff Easley hunched over his easel, painting away with a look of intense concentration. Occasionally I would wander up there and find some aspect of the DRAGONLANCE world gradually evolving amid the smell of turpentine and paint rags.

DRAGONLANCE at this stage was at something of a turning point. In 1995 *Dragons of a Summer Flame* had ended the Fourth Age and initiated the Age of Mortals. Weis and Hickman, as far as anyone knew, had no plans to write further novels. A design team at TSR was in the process of developing a new game system for the world, called SAGA®.

Over the next nine months, two things changed decisively. The first was that Washington-based Wizards of the Coast bought TSR. The head of WotC, Peter Adkison, came to Lake Geneva and walked the halls, energizing staff members with his cheerfulness and vitality. Peter was an unabashed fan of roleplaying and TSR, always ready to plunge into an all-night session of DUNGEONS & DRAGONS®.

The second event occurred in the interval between WotC's purchase of TSR and our move from Lake Geneva to Renton, Washington. Margaret and Tracy told Peter they had an idea they wanted to pitch to him and to the Book Department. We had no notion of what this idea was, but we were pretty sure, given Margaret and Tracy's evident enthusiasm, that it would be important.

Margaret, Don Perrin, and Tracy arrived at TSR early in the morning. Over coffee and donuts we exchanged small talk, then moved into a conference room for their presentation. At one end of a long, glass-topped table, Tracy hunched over his laptop, poring over his notes for the meeting, while Don and Margaret leaned forward in their chairs, a few scribbled pages in front of them. They explained to the small group of us gathered that morning their idea for a new DRAGONLANCE series called The War of Souls.

"It begins," Tracy observed, "with a kender and a time-travel device."

When they finished the presentation, there was a moment of silence as we absorbed what we'd heard. It was followed by a babble of voices, as we began throwing out ideas on how we could make this proposal happen. Peter Adkison sat quietly listening to us, a huge grin on his face.

Amid the transition from Wisconsin to Washington in the summer of 1997, Mary Kirchoff returned to the company to head the Book Department. Under her leadership the War of Souls project moved forward. Margaret and Tracy came to Renton for several productive brainstorming sessions on the nature of the new series. At the same time, the game designers gradually moved DRAGONLANCE back from SAGA to the more successful D&D® system.

While waiting for the draft of *Dragons of a Fallen Sun*, the first book in the new storyline, we launched several short series designed to fill in gaps between the Chaos War, described in *Dragons of Summer Flame*, and the latter part of the Fifth Age in which the War of Souls was set. The Chaos War Series and the Bridges of Time series allowed us to try out some new directions for design and art work.

In 1999, while looking at proposed covers for *Dragons of a Fallen Sun*, we came across the work of Matt Stawicki. It seemed to fit perfectly with the direction we'd decided we wanted to go. We wanted to show more of the world of Krynn, to focus on setting as well as character. Matt's magnificent painting of Mina before the city of Sanction fulfilled this requirement beyond our dreams.

DRAGONLANCE art has continued the high standards set by this piece. New artists such as Mark Zug, Daniel Horne, Todd Lockwood, and Jerry Vander Stelt have joined their efforts to older artists such as Jeff Easley, Brom, Clyde Caldwell, Larry Elmore, and others. The result has been not merely a continuation of DRAGONLANCE but a progression.

Now, as the War of Souls draws to a close, we can look back on almost twenty years of DRAGONLANCE. It is a remarkable saga. I'm proud to have been associated with it.

MATT
Stawicki

Born and raised in the Wilmington, Delaware, area, young Matt Stawicki found Saturday morning superhero cartoons irresistible and credits them for his interest in the fantastic. As he got older, his interests broadened somewhat. Barbarians, gladiators, and exotic, extraterrestrial worlds started to become the focus of his art.

The paintings of noted illustrators such as N.C. Wyeth, Norman Rockwell, and Maxfield Parrish are among his greatest influences. He is also a big film fan, and movies form a continual source of inspired imagery.

After graduating from the Pennsylvania School of Art & Design, Matt chose to stay in Pennsylvania where he spent a year or so painting and studying the illustration field. During this time he began to understudy with western painter Ken Laager, whom Matt considers "instrumental in my learning not only the craft of painting but also the professionalism necessary to survive in the illustration field.

"Although I consider myself a classically trained painter, I am influenced by the wonderful work and technological advancements currently taking place in the illustration field. In the last few years I have moved to doing most of my work digitally. I find the digital medium more suited to commercial work due to its flexibility. The physical problems with painting—what's dry, what's wet—are no longer an issue. I can be 'reckless' when working out ideas, which allows me to experiment a lot more.

"However," Stawicki is quick to note, "the computer does not create art, nor does it make obsolete the traditional ways of doing things. It is merely a tool. I have found that the same craft and attention to composition must be present for the artwork to succeed no matter what the medium."

Matt currently resides in Delaware.

DRAGONLANCE Chronicles

Notice the seasonal tones throughout each work—warm oranges and reds for autumn, bleak and cold blue for winter, and vibrant, rich green for spring. "That's very much on purpose," says Stawicki. "The palettes were definitely a big part in giving these pieces the feel each one needed.

"I really like doing the big defining landscape of the world just as much as the characters. To me, that's just as important in conveying convincing fantasy. Movies like Star Wars have taken developing the environment to a very high level. This influences what we want to see in illustration. I feel the world can be just as much a character as the figures.

DRAGONS OF AUTUMN TWILIGHT

"This is the tree house of my dreams. If I was an eccentric
millionaire and I designed a tree house, this would be it.
Kind of Robinson Crusoe inspired."

DRAGONS OF WINTER NIGHT

"The art director sent me black and white photocopies from the old *Dragonlance Atlas* by Karen Wynn Fonstad, which inspired the architecture here. The castle had to look a certain way because of that, but I had some leeway in the view we had."

DRAGONS OF SPRING DAWNING

"Caramon and Raistlin here were modified from live
models, but Kitiara in the background was developed
more from a series of drawings."

DRAGONLANCE LEGENDS

We see the city of Istar, a bleak, craggy castle by night, and the portal to the Abyss. "The change in motif from the Chronicles was totally unintentional," says Stawicki. "It just worked out that the environments we wanted to show seemed to be more architectural, but in hindsight I think it works rather nicely."

war of the twins

Notice the distant griffins by the moon. This is a favorite technique of Stawicki's to establish perspective, distance, and scale.

TEST OF THE TWINS

Notice the change in Raistlin from the first piece.
Whereas he had been holding, almost caressing
Crysania, now he is turning away. It is up to Caramon
to save her. Raistlin's loyalties are decided, and
Crysania has been cast off.

THE WAR OF SOULS

The color motif—red, blue, green—repeats the Chronicles covers. "Again, this was sheer coincidence," says Stawicki. "I wasn't trying to tie in to Chronicles so much as give each piece its own appropriate color palette. I like to let the subject help define what the palette should be.

"With most art orders, I just get a synopsis with specific character information. With War of Souls, I had the opportunity to read the books, which really helped in defining the characters."

DRAGONS OF A FALLEN SUN

"This was the first DRAGONLANCE painting I ever did. This horse was also a character, so I wanted to outfit him as well as Mina. The mountains are almost entirely drawn from imagination, though I did build a small model that created a guide to show me how the light would affect the rocks being lit strongly from below."

Dragons of a Lost Star

"This is another one of my favorite DRAGONLANCE pieces. The ectoplasmic ghosts and ghoulies were something I'd wanted to do for a while. I love doing skeleton warriors, and this was my chance to do a big parade of them. I wanted to spread it across as much of the image as I could, but I also think it helps give impact to the figures. Goldmoon can see and talk to the ghosts, which I tried to convey in her pose, but Gerard is unaware of them. I also wanted to show that she was not afraid of the ghosts. I thought one them bowing to her in a chivalrous manner could be just what it needed. It also goes to show you that skeleton warriors have manners too."

DRAGONS OF A VANISHED MOON

"In the original sketch, the skulls were human skulls, then I found out they were supposed to be dragon skulls. This created some challenges since the composition was originally crafted with rounded skulls, whereas dragons have sharper skulls."

THE AGE OF MORTALS

The Age of Mortals series was somewhat of a departure for Stawicki thematically. Whereas Chronicles, Legends, and the War of Souls are major trilogies with an ongoing storyline, each book in the Age of Mortals is intended to stand on its own. This allowed Stawicki to give each piece a look of its own.

conundrum

"I love this piece. This was an opportunity where the art order came down and we really weren't sure how to handle this. When I was younger, my family traveled throughout the U.S., to various national parks like Goblin Valley and the deserts of Utah, so I had seen these various formations. Many of the Native Americans would name these great rock formations after the animals they resembled, which inspired me to make the background arch resemble a dragon."

THE LIONESS

"A hunting party. I always like playing with natural sunlight as a way of spotlighting figures. I'm a huge KISS fan, and Kerian's war paint in this piece is a modified version of Ace Freeley's make-up."

DARK THANE

"Dwarves aren't comical to me. I see them as being intense—little Vikings, very Norse-looking. I really like this piece for the impact that the flesh tones, the light, and the spotlight effect given to the main character. Kind of reminiscent of the more neutral Frazetta pieces, whom I am constantly influenced by."

THE SEARCH FOR MAGIC

"This is one of the more unique ones I've done for DRAGONLANCE because it isn't a scene. Being a collection of short stories, the book lent itself to the montage/movie poster approach. I look toward what's going to give it visual impact, more of a design approach as opposed to a storytelling approach."

second Generation

"I wanted the color to suggest rebirth. One of my favorite things about this piece is the birds. It helps to establish light and scale so that the background doesn't look lifeless. I always try to create just as much on the back wrap as the front. You want these places to look like some place you'd want to be or go on vacation."

Dragons of summer Flame

"Here with Tanis was my first shot at aging a character. That was kind of neat—a character I'd done before, so I felt I knew him pretty well. With these characters, there's already something established. These are beloved characters. In Usha's case, I wasn't told she had this exact outfit, but I was told she had a Middle Eastern ensemble. When I do dragons, there are some times when I sculpt a head and photograph it or work from the model itself. This was one where I made a sculpture."

MARK ZUG

Mark Zug has been drawing for as long as he can remember. At a very early age he discovered the power of pencil and paper to bring things to life—especially dinosaurs, superheroes, Jules-Vernean submarines, imaginary cars, races of ancient astronauts, and starships inspired by then-fresh *Star Trek*. As a teen Zug turned to literature for inspiration, discovering Frank Herbert and Tolkien. Giving his art a break after high school, he worked his way up to class-A machinist at a nearby factory while he flirted with a musical career.

Zug returned to art under the fresh inspiration of Frank Frazetta and illustrators of the Brandywine School, putting himself through art school as well as ghost-painting western novel covers and penciling historical comic strips on the side. His first big break came illustrating Harlan Ellison's *I, Robot* screenplay, for which he also did 160 pages of fully painted comics. He fulfilled a long-held dream illustrating Frank Herbert's Dune universe in the form of Last Unicorn's collectible card game, which proved a springboard into the burgeoning world of gaming. To date his work has appeared on the covers of *Popular Science, Dragon®, Dungeon®, Duelist®, Inquest, Star Wars Gamer,* and *Amazing Stories magazines.* From there, he went on to grace the covers of novels by Tanith Lee, the DRAGONLANCE world, and on many products for Shadowrun, Battletech, and MAGIC: THE GATHERING®. He was nominated for a Chesley and received the Jack Gaughan Award for Best Emerging Artist in 2001.

Though always committed to illustration, his ambitions are wider. "A friend of mine in Manhattan, named Pedro Boregaard, makes jewelry. I advise you to look him up. Under his hands materials transform into shapes both dazzling and grand, with a rugged pull on the subconscious. From a figment in his mind he makes them and sells directly to the special customer who can't do without it. This is exactly what I want to do with my art."

Mark invites all and sundry to visit his website, www.markzug.com, with wishes of peace and a great view.

"This was the first DRAGONLANCE piece I did. A peculiarity of the Crossroads series is that often the story is not even written when the art is commissioned, which is a mixed blessing: I miss out on the inspiration of a good writer, but I have a lot of liberty with designing the characters and props. In this case, all I knew was that Linsha Majere had short red hair, dressed like a knight, and had an owl. Her armor I cobbled from a host of aristocratic designs of the fifteenth century and later. This cover hit my heroic reflexes right away because a female knight cannot avoid the Joan of Arc association, and the very first sketch I did is what I used."

"In this piece, Lucy is beautifully described by author Mary Herbert. At the time of the story, the famous light-tower of Flotsam had been destroyed and its harbor traffic decimated, in spite of the intact, thriving port city we see in my painting."

The Thieves' Guild

"On *The Thieves' Guild* I was mighty proud of placing the viewer in the cliffs off to the northwest of Palanthas so that you had a good view of the palace, the northwest and northeast towered gates, and the Tower of High Sorcery. Unfortunately the Tower of High Sorcery wasn't there anymore, nor is the enchanted forest still visible just beyond the elf hero's left knee. And I think I would have lit the city with a bit less zeal had I known that its golden age had passed. It points up one of the challenges of DRAGONLANCE for me: I have never followed the books, yet it is so richly imagined that I want to show it in a kind of resplendence that may or may not fit the individual story."

The Dragon Isles

"This was a highly enjoyable cover for me. I got to design a mer-woman, as well as an undersea city that wasn't constrained by a map. In fidelity to the story concept, I tried to infuse a pre-Classical Minoan flavor to the architecture while skewing the horizontal surfaces enough to show the irrelevance of floors to a race that swims. As it is being steadily ruined and fractured by volcanic action, the whole effect is a kind of tumbled-down grandiosity that is one of my very favorite backgrounds."

Brom

Born on March 9, 1965, in Albany, Georgia, Brom is the son of an Army aviator. He spent his school years on the move, living in such places as Japan, Alabama, and Hawaii, and graduated from high school in Frankfurt, Germany. From his earliest memories he has been obsessed with the creation of the weird, the monstrous, and the beautiful.

At the age of twenty, Brom started working full-time as a commercial illustrator. By twenty-one, he had two national art representatives and was doing work for Coke, IBM, Columbia Pictures, and CNN. Three years later Brom entered the fantasy field he had loved all his life when TSR hired him full-time, and he began to introduce his personal vision of fantasy to the worlds of TSR. He spent the next three years creating the look and feel of the best-selling Dark Sun® world.

In 1993, Brom returned to the freelance market. Since then he has been working feverishly on hundreds of paintings for every facet of the genre, from novels (Michael Moorcock, Terry Brooks, R.A. Salvatore, E.R. Burroughs), roleplaying (TSR, White Wolf, FASA, Wizards of the Coast), comics (DC, Chaos, Dark Horse), games (Doom2, Diablo2, Heretic, Sega, Activision), and films (Tim Burton's *Sleepy Hollow*, *Galaxy Quest*, *Bless the Child*, *Ghosts of Mars*, and *Scooby Doo*).

Brom's powerful and haunting visions can be found collected in his two art books *Darkwerks* and *Offerings*, both available from Paper Tiger.

Brom resides with his family in the Seattle area. There he is ever painting, writing, and trying to reach a happy sing-a-long with the many demons dancing about in his head.

"The world of Dragonlance was well developed by the time I arrived on the scene. The key characters and the look and feel were long established by some of the top artists in the business. The challenge for me was to contribute something of my own to this fantastic setting.

"From the first I aimed for assignments that contained characters or elements that had not previously been illustrated, since a large part of my love of art comes from creating and bringing to life visions from my imagination."

For more information on Brom please visit www.BromArt.com

"This is not only the first painting I contributed to DRAGONLANCE but also one of my first attempts to paint with oils."

The Messenger

"Most covers are about conflict, so it was interesting to paint a cover that was more about conveying a mood rather than action."

"Keeping in the graphic theme of having strong singular color palette for each of these books, I played off the title and went for a golden glow amongst the happy carnage of dead trolls."

"Here we have the orge lord searching for his destiny amongst the cold foothills."

Taladas, The Minotaurs

"The fog adds that much-needed touch of tension as the minotaur stalks (or is he being stalked?) amongst the foggy standing stones."

DANIEL Horne

Born on June 3, 1960, in Pittsburgh, Pennsylvania, Daniel Horne showed from an early age a passion for storytelling in art. The mystical paintings and sculptures of the Catholic Church were his first experience with the wonders of storytelling art. Then came the films of Ray Harryhausen—fantasies made real, creatures that lived and breathed. All had a profound impact on him.

In 1978 Daniel had the good fortune to study with noted historical painter and sixth-generation Howard Pyle student, Ken Laager, who taught Daniel to "throw your heart into your painting and leap in after it," to "make your characters flesh and blood with a past, a history, not a cardboard stand-up to drape a costume on." Daniel has stayed true to Howard Pyle's teachings in the fantasy characters he has painted over the past twenty years.

Since 1982, Daniel has produced over 300 fantasy novel covers, 170 dust jackets, and dozens of magazine and roleplaying game covers.

This award-winning painter and sculptor lives in Cherry Hill, New Jersey, with his wife, Joy, daughter, Jen, and son, Andy. When not painting and sculpting, Daniel can be found hanging out with his family, and he is the goalie for the Jersey Juggernauts hockey team.

"I've been an illustrator for twenty years now. I was trained as an oil painter, and I'll die as an oil painter. There is beauty of mixing the colors, applying the paint. . . . I could never stop doing that. It's how I feel I express myself best. I love the physical aspects of painting—applying the paint, creating the atmosphere and the mood. Nothing has really changed in 500 years, and I get this really cool sense of belonging because my materials are the same. I do appreciate the guys who do the computer stuff. There's some really beautiful stuff out there, but it's just not for me. This is just my chosen medium."

"The best depiction of this tragic family. This is my favorite piece in this book." —Robert Campbell, graphic designer
"Not only is this my favorite piece in this book, it is my all-time favorite DRAGONLANCE *painting."* —Mark Sehestedt, editor

"There's a history of artists who went before me. At first, it was intimidating, because these characters are such icons. After I got over my initial fear, I just decided to do the paintings, to make the characters seem alive, give them emotion, and make it real—from the light to the blowing wind. I want these characters to seem like living, breathing people with histories, lives, and emotions. I chose the lighting to evoke the feeling of the sky after a storm—the shadows are cutting across to emphasize that things have come and passed.

"The art director wanted Kitiara in the background, but at this point in the story she hadn't actually met the guys yet. How am I going to solve this problem? I didn't want to make her tiny. I wanted her to have just as much cover space as the guys, so I put her outside this sort of bistro, hanging out on the veranda. The characters are each in their own world."

"I had to do two versions of this painting, because in the writing the book changed from the initial art order. There was no longer a scene of an ogre fighting a draconian in the story, so I didn't feel right about having one on the cover.

"In the first version, the guy who modeled for all the characters is the Fire Chief of Cherry Hill, New Jersey."

"Like all my art, this piece is all character driven. I don't specialize in big vistas or huge interior scenes. I love developing the characters. The art director wanted all the characters in a pitched battle, so I arranged the composition in a way to get the most of the characters and show the emotional impact of going into a battle. I wanted viewers to feel like participants rather than viewers."

"This painting invariably draws the biggest response from people. I think I excel most when given the least amount of direction. I was told we have a beautiful woman, who is blind, a gray-and-black tiger with a rune symbol on his forehead, and they are in a palace. I didn't want to do the same old castle, so I put her in a sort of arboretum just for something different, more exotic, and interesting. I wanted it to be as atmospheric as I could."

LOCKWOOD

TODD

Before joining the Wizards of the Coast art staff in September of '96, Todd Lockwood was a sixteen-year veteran of advertising, with agents in Denver and New York.

"After painting my two-hundredth dewdrop on my fiftieth can of Coors, I realized I had to get out. I was literally ready to leave illustration altogether. I was that burned out. I stumbled into fantasy illustration almost by accident, but I knew right then that I could do this. I started attending fantasy conventions and met with other artists like Michael Whelan, who was a huge help to me, very supportive, offering advice and suggestions."

Since then, Todd's work has appeared on the covers of numerous books, magazines, and game products and on playing cards for Wizards of the Coast, on the covers of *Asimov's* and *Analog*, and in the pages of *Science Fiction Age* and *Realms of Fantasy*. Among the honors his artwork has received are two World Fantasy Artshow awards, several Chesleys, and many appearances in the Spectrum art anthologies.

Todd lives in Washington State with his wife, and three children.

"This picture ended up very different from its original conception. It was supposed to have been a silver and a red dragon against a nighttime sky. At the last minute, the art order changed the silver to a blue, which wouldn't have shown up very well against a night sky, so Todd changed to a warmer 'sunset'-colored sky."

This was the second job Todd did for TSR, and it was the piece that got him hired as a staff artist. Every figure in the painting is Todd. He made the lead figure more rugged, so that people often tell him it looks like Sean Connery. "Actually, it looks like my dad with long hair."

That lead knight on the run is David LaForce, also known as "Diesel," one of the cartographers at TSR. Todd wanted to convey the gargantuan size of DRAGONLANCE's dragon overlords. There's nothing to do against one of these guys but run.

The Last Thane

"I wanted a dwarf who looked like he could kick your ass."

Silver Dragon

This was done for the cover of DRAGON Magazine.

CLYDE CALDWELL

For more than twenty years, fantasy artist Clyde Caldwell has been a prominent figure in the field of fantastic illustration. His portrayal of strong, sexy female characters has been his hallmark from the beginning. Caldwell's covers for major book publishers, *Heavy Metal Magazine*, Marvel Comics, and roleplaying game publishers have established him as a fan favorite, both in this country and abroad.

With hundreds of fantasy and science fiction paintings under his belt, his images have been reproduced in the form of posters, limited edition prints, puzzles, calendars, sculptures, portfolios, trading cards, and more.

Savage Hearts: The Clyde Caldwell Sketchbook, Volume 1 was released in 1997 by SQ Productions. Volume 2 is planned for release in 2002. A full-color art book is also in the works and is slated for publication in the summer of 2002.

"One of the things that drew me to the DRAGONLANCE saga from the beginning was the writers' development of interesting characters. Since my art is primarily character driven, I was excited at the prospect of helping to visualize the varied and highly individualized characters created by Hickman, Weis, and company."

"Here Tanis and Flint guard each others' backs, foreshadowing the deep friendship that develops between the two characters and carries them through many an adventure. It was strange depicting Tanis without his signature beard."

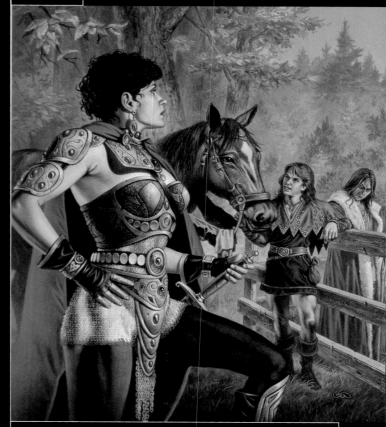

"I remember having a tight deadline for this painting, so I roughed in the background very quickly and spontaneously, intending to go back in and tighten it up when I was finished with the figures in the foreground. Time didn't permit my doing this, but in the end I was rather pleased with the looser approach."

Steel & Stone

"While I was trying to show the tension between a young Tanis Half-Elven and Kitiara in this scene, one of my favorite parts of the painting is the mountains in the background. The subtle solidity and strength in those mountains seem to echo the theme of an unstoppable force meeting an immovable object."

"For the background of this painting I chose the ruins of Xak Tsaroth. I first painted this underground city in an earlier work, *Dragons of Despair*."

"The dragon skull in this painting was thrown in almost as an afterthought. Though there were no dragons in Krynn during the time this story took place, I felt that the skull hinted at the fact that dragons had indeed existed, and was a portent of their return."

JEFF easLey

"I've been drawing since I was three or four years old," says Jeff Easley. "I just sort of moved toward majoring in art in college as a natural progression. I had always been into fantasy and science fiction. I was a big monster fan early on. My interest waned somewhat as I grew older, but was rekindled in college as I really had to decide what I wanted to do. I was out of college and doing what little freelance work I could muster when I learned that Larry Elmore, whom I had met through a mutual friend, had accepted a job at TSR. I learned from Larry that they were expanding and looking for more artists, so I applied and was hired on. That was a little over twenty years ago, now.

"I recall that when TSR decided to do a Dragonlance calendar, the first three novels hadn't hit yet. When the calendar came out for 1985, Dragonlance had not yet developed a following, so sales were low and returns were high. The next year at Gen Con, TSR was giving away the calendars at the TSR booth. A couple of guys from Canada snagged several boxes and had all the guys in the calendar sign every plate. By that time, Dragonlance was starting to catch on, and the Canadian guys told us the '85 calendar was selling for $50.00 a piece in Canada."

Jeff is happy to have been so involved in the Dragonlance setting. "Being involved with Dragonlance from the beginning has been a very satisfying and creative experience. I consider it a privilege to have been given this opportunity to conceptualize a small part of the Dragonlance world. It is most certainly an honor to have my efforts included among the uniformly excellent work of my peers (and betters) in this book."

"I really tried to get in there and get some subtle things going, kind of like some old-fashioned salon portrait."

The original idea behind the Bertrem's Guides was to do for Ansalon what Daniel Pool did for nineteenth-century English literature in his book *What Jane Austen Ate and Charles Dickens Knew*. In this painting, Jeff gives us a picture of a ruler paying tribute to one of the minions of the great dragon overlords of the Fifth Age.

"It's always fun to get the chance to do something a little unusual like say . . . a great stone dragon."

New Beginnings

"I read the Greek myths over and over when I was young. I always thought minotaurs were pretty cool."

"Big battle scenes can work well if you can manage to maintain a strong focal point."

"I had a lot of fun painting that big gooey egg."

"I don't often get a chance to paint nice-looking ladies, so this was a bit of a diversion."

The Gates of Thorbardin

"I always kind of liked the way the ethereal dwarf king turned out."

"Sometimes a limited color treatment works well."

"The DRAGONLANCE characters make for interesting covers,
especially when you do one with the distinctive DRAGONLANCE armor."

"I'm pretty sure this is my only giant octopus attack painting to date."

"My main recollection of this painting was having a very short deadline in which to finish it."

"There aren't too many ways you can go wrong with an epic dragon battle."

LARRY ELMORE

Larry Elmore has been creating fantasy and science fiction art for over twenty years. From 1981 to 1987 he worked as a staff artist for TSR, Inc., where he helped set the standards for art in the roleplaying genre. Besides creating covers for DUNGEONS & DRAGONS, AD&D®, and other gaming books and scenarios, he is probably best known for his work in the world of DRAGONLANCE.

"The first DRAGONLANCE paintings I ever did were around 1985 for a calendar. While we were working on the calendar, the book line started up, so I had to jump on them immediately. I kind of became the de facto art director for DRAGONLANCE for a while. People still love DRAGONLANCE as much today as they did twenty years ago. It's amazing, because when we started no one thought it was going to be that big of a deal, but it's still here, stronger than ever."

It usually takes Elmore about two weeks to finish a painting. "What slows me down these days are computers. The website does great business, but between e-mails, phone calls, art orders, interviews, and correspondence, I've had to hire a full-time secretary. I've had to almost become an art director again, but I want to be an artist. I actually have to make time to paint now!"

Elmore paints exclusively in oils, on either canvass or masonite board. He has used models for years and still continues to do so on a fairly regular basis. "A few years ago I advertised and got a great crop of models, but I tend to use mostly locals. I hang out at Wal-Mart and just ask people if they would like to pose for a picture. Where I live in Kentucky is a lot like Mayberry, so finding enough willing participants is sometimes tough."

Since 1987, Elmore has been working as a freelance illustrator, doing covers for comics, computer games, magazines, and fantasy and science fiction books. He is also the co-author of *Runes of Autumn* and creator of the Sovereign Stone series.

"When I first did this piece, we'd never really had too many images of a dragonrider. This was a pretty quick painting. In fact, when DRAGONLANCE took off, everything was a get-it-done-quick painting. I was just trying to show a complete dragon with a rider, and I wanted to capture the feeling of being up in the air."

"It was shortly after this painting that I had a stroke. I was putting out a lot of paintings at the time—maybe two or three a month—and I was working myself to death. The stroke was on the right side of the brain, which is the creative side. After the stroke, I went through a period (in the mid '90s) when a lot of my work suffered because of it. I thought my career was over, but it took about three years to get back to producing work I was satisfied with."

"I made the girl long because I knew the title treatment they were using at the time had to run along the bottom as well as the top, and I didn't want type going across her belly. Everything here is made up except the girl. She's the same model who was in The Dargonesti."

"The concepting of this piece was done the old-fashioned way. Michael Williams, the author, just came over and talked to me about the story, and we went from there. I tried to capture the feeling of immediate danger. The kid looks scared, and the Knight is watching something. The trick with this Knight was to make him a Knight without having him look like Sturm.

"See the snake on the fallen tree? Most people miss that."

"This was one I did after my full recovery. Parts of this painting I really, really like—the room, the whole set-up, all the light coming from candles. Of course, it's more light than three candles would produce, but maybe they're magical candles. At the time I painted this, I was actually trying to get away from DRAGONLANCE, broaden my horizons a bit, but I really wanted to do a good job for Margaret. Still, to this day, I wish I could have redone Raistlin. The guy I had pose for Raistlin was just too big. Raistlin looks healthy as a horse here, which is all wrong for the character. He should have been frail and sickly, so I call this piece 'The Healthy Raistlin.'"

"This was back in the old days when we didn't do much preparation. We just started painting to get it done. The art director wanted to show both the inside and the outside of the cave, which was really difficult."

"I like this painting, particularly the path leading to the crystal mountain in an ethereal-type landscape—very dreamy. I made the gate design myself. I wanted it to look beautiful, but I didn't want it to hide the mountain. You could actually crawl through this gate; it's more symbolic, not meant to keep you out."

"This is one of my favorite DRAGONLANCE pieces. I had never painted an underwater painting before. I'm such a landlocked person. I've never even been under the sea, so I had to totally fake this. I used a very beautiful model named Shonda for the girl. She had to lean against a chair to look like she was floating. The guy is simply made up.

"I had no idea what coral looked like underwater. This was the first year I was online, so I looked up some websites and printed out pictures of some coral, but they were so bad that I eventually threw 'em away and just faked it. About a year later, some people came up to me at Dragon Con and wanted to talk about this because they were divers. I thought, 'They're going to tear me apart,' but they said, 'We wanted to tell you how accurate you were—the coral is amazing. The one thing you missed was the bubbles.' But hey, these are sea elves, so they're probably breathing water, not air."

Night of the Eye

"This was on canvas. Of course, because of the title and the content of the book itself, the moons line up to look like an eyeball.

"It's always challenging to do a night scene, and this piece was where I was trying to get more on track with doing them. The bright moon giving all the light really helped. A lot of people doing night scenes tend to make the sky really dark blue or black, and they get it too dark. I used to do the same thing. You can't make the sky too dark, because then everything else has to be even darker."

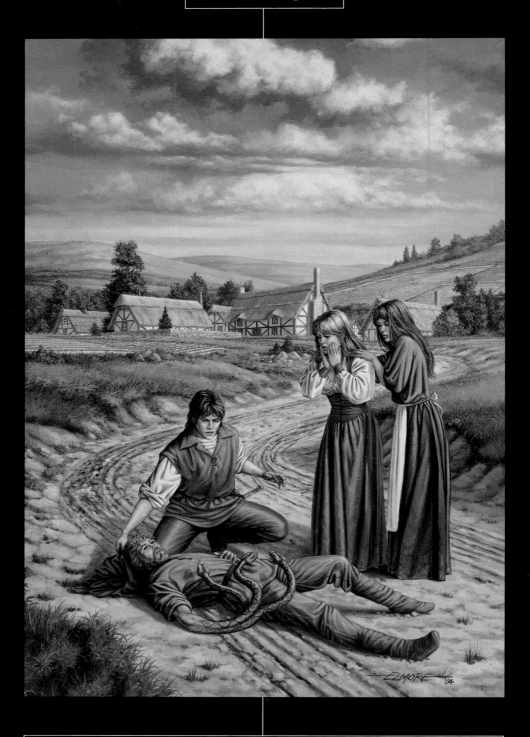

"When I did this cover I started trying to paint on canvass again, which gave me a looser style. Where I had my fun was the landscape itself. I just really love the background of this piece. It reminded me of little villages I saw while driving through Germany. I had one model who posed for both of these girls in this picture. It's also the same guy posing for the dead guy and the live guy."

"I had to do this one pretty quick. My daughter posed for the young guy on the left. The dwarf and the others were just out of my imagination. I was trying to get away from the bright, bright colors, which seemed to be what TSR was pushing in the early years. It got to the point where it was like eating candy every day, so here I was trying to swing back to the other way.

"I had been out west and I photographed the Rockies, which inspired the background in this painting."

"In this piece, the art directors couldn't decide what they wanted to do with Kitiara. They didn't know if they wanted Kitiara there as a ghost or a real person, so I left her feet a little weird-looking, which always bugged me. I really like the dragon and the guy though."

"This was also done during my recovery. I had to keep a schedule just to make a living, but I wasn't as fast as I used to be, and every painting was a struggle. This was a foggy, gray, nightmare period for me. I had to rush to make this deadline.

"The art director wanted the figures peeking from behind a rock, which posed a problem because I didn't want to paint just the back of their heads."

"Goldmoon and the Plainsmen being modeled after Native Americans was originally from Margaret, but I added in the feathers and beads. Their clothing designs were sort of a combination of Celtic design with Native American stuff.

"This was during my 'big eye' period. I was told the elves have big eyes, and it began to creep into all my art. The other artists really gave me a hard time about it. I really had to work to get rid of the big eye problem. Of course, now with the popularity of animé, that kind of stuff is in style."

"I like Tasslehoff in this one. The only model I used for any of these Chronicles covers was an old photo of a girl that I used for Kitiara in this piece."

"I wasn't into Raistlin back then much. After reading the books, I was
pissed at him and at Caramon for not kicking his brother and going on.
It's only in recent years that I've really gotten into the character. The
idea of having Raistlin in shadow for this piece was Margaret's idea."

"My daughter posed for Goldmoon in this piece. This is the last time I ever painted Goldmoon. The draconian here is patterned after Keith Parkinson's draconian in the fantastic painting 'What do you mean we're lost?' "

"The stream and trees here are a real place, just about two or three miles from my place. The bottom part is intentionally blank to leave room for the author's name and such. The minotaurs' heads were from some statues of a bull I have."

Jerry VANDER STELT

"Ever since my early years in school," say Jerry Vander Stelt, "I have always had a pencil in my hand and my head in the clouds. Much to my teachers' annoyance, my grades were lacking (due mostly to boredom and a lack of interest). My desire to become an illustrator hit home after reading C.S. Lewis' Chronicles of Narnia for the first time. My love of the genre was forged all the stronger after reading J.R.R. Tolkien's *The Lord of the Rings* and *The Hobbit*.

"I got started by sending samples to various publishers and art representatives, and then paying close attention to their comments or suggestions. Once I felt my portfolio was ready, I sent out my latest pieces and started to get responses. I never had any formal training, but I wish to use my talents and skills in a positive way in this industry.

"My paintings are rendered in acrylic paints on illustration board. Acrylic dries fast, allowing for quick layering. I use traditional techniques along with airbrush. Typically, after several rough thumbnail sketches for myself, I submit a more polished sketch for the art director. From there, we discuss possible changes or alterations, then proceed with the final art."

THE DHAMON SAGA

Downfall

"For each of these covers in the Dhamon Saga, I wanted to take the reader and show the mood, color, geography, and maybe even a little history of the DRAGONLANCE world."

Betrayal

"DRAGONLANCE gave me a broad range in which I could explore and delve, allowing for interesting imagery to rise to the surface. As with all my cover work, I try to be accurate to the story and characters. I hope my ideas of this world and its characters are ones that will make the reader revert back to the cover and say, 'Yeah, that's just how I envisioned it!'"

Redemption

"I use photo reference for the characters. My style is photorealistic, so I need to be able to pick up all the little nuances in the human form. The model here is me, posing as Dhamon—along with some adjustments, such as hair and more muscle! I did not realize I would be doing two other pieces in the series following the first book, or I would have found another model. Oh, well."

CONTRIBUTING ARTISTS

This was the cover of the 1997 DRAGONLANCE anthology of short stories. One of the defining characteristics of the Fifth Age is the dragon overlords—massive monsters far larger and more powerful than Krynn has ever seen before. Note the sheer size of the dragon. He has an entire tower in the grasp of one claw!

"Kicks ass!" —Ryan Sansaver, art director

Though this was technically the cover for a novel in the RAVENLOFT®
setting, Lord Soth is such an integral part of DRAGONLANCE and
McCann's piece is so stunning that we had to include it. The original
idea for the painting was to do a cover reminiscent of John Berendt's
Midnight in the Garden of Good and Evil—more menacing than terrifying.

"When I was a child of ten," says McCann, "I wandered off whilst
attending a funeral with my family and got lost for about half an hour
in this huge Victorian cemetery. It was winter and one of those
brooding dark cloudy days we so often get here in England, and I soon
found myself in the oldest part of the graveyard. I was very frightened
by the weathered monuments and broken statues that looked as if any
second they could come to life and grab me. I tried to get that same
feeling into this painting. For me at least it worked."

With his brother Greg, Tim Hildebrandt rose to fame in the late
1970s when their artwork filled the pages of the Tolkien calendars.
In the early '90s, Tim put his skills to work in DRAGONLANCE,
creating the covers for the entire Dwarven Nations trilogy.

The Doom Brigade
by Keith Parkinson

"This was my first cover for Dragonlance. I was excited to work on it—the first painting I ever copied was a Dragonlance cover by Keith Parkinson!

"I normally read a book to approach a cover, but in this case the book wasn't finished, so I spent some time discussing ideas with the art director and then submitted some sketches for approval. It was important to show the two protagonists in the glory of their city, side by side, yet not facing each other, as a foreshadowing of things to come. Since there is an arc to the story that will be revealed in the following books, we were looking at it as part one of a three-part illustration. The greatest challenge for me was capturing the architecture. For this, I looked to the art of Alma-Tadema, as well as books with European and Middle Eastern structures."